ROOT, Phyllis

Flip, flap, fly!

Flip, Flap, Fly!

Phyllis Root

illustrated by David Walker

WALKER BOOKS
AND SUBSIDIARIES

LONDON · BOSTON · SYDNEY · AUCKLAND

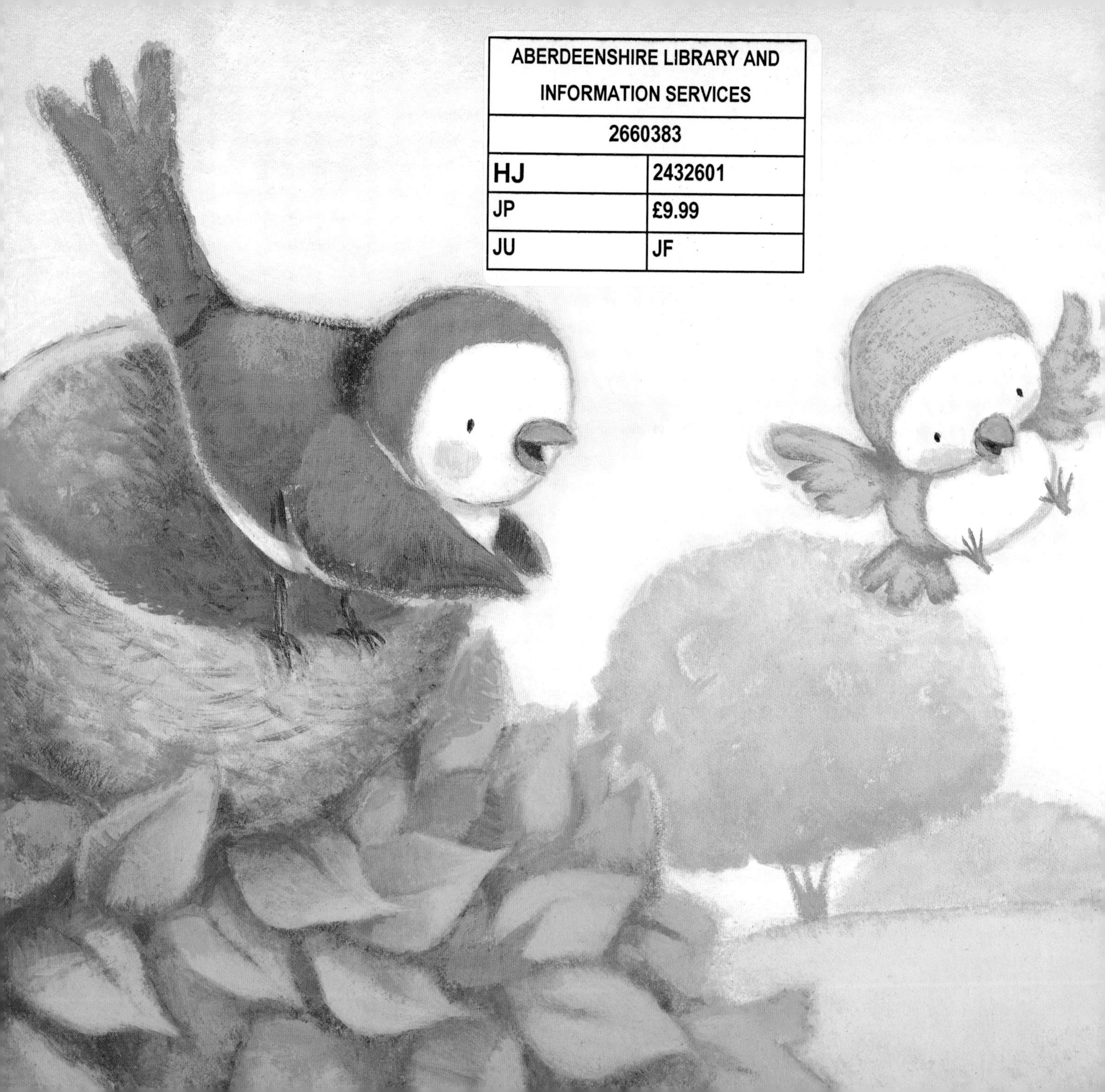

"Fly!" cheeps the baby bird.
"Way up high!"
So the mama helps the baby bird
flip

flap

fly

in the blue, blue sky,
where the wind blows *whish*.

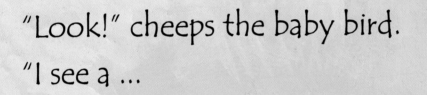

"Look!" cheeps the baby bird.
"I see a ...

"FISH!"

"Swim!" blurps the baby fish.
"Deep down dim."
So the mama helps the baby fish
splish

splash

swim

through the weeds and the reeds
in the green, green lake.

"Look!" blurps the baby fish.
"I see a ...

"SNAKE!"

"Wiggle!" hisses baby snake.
"Wiggle with a squiggle!"
So the mama helps the baby snake
ziggle

zaggle

wiggle

in the brown, brown sand
where the sun shines hotter.

"Look!" hisses baby snake.
"I see an ...

"OTTER!"

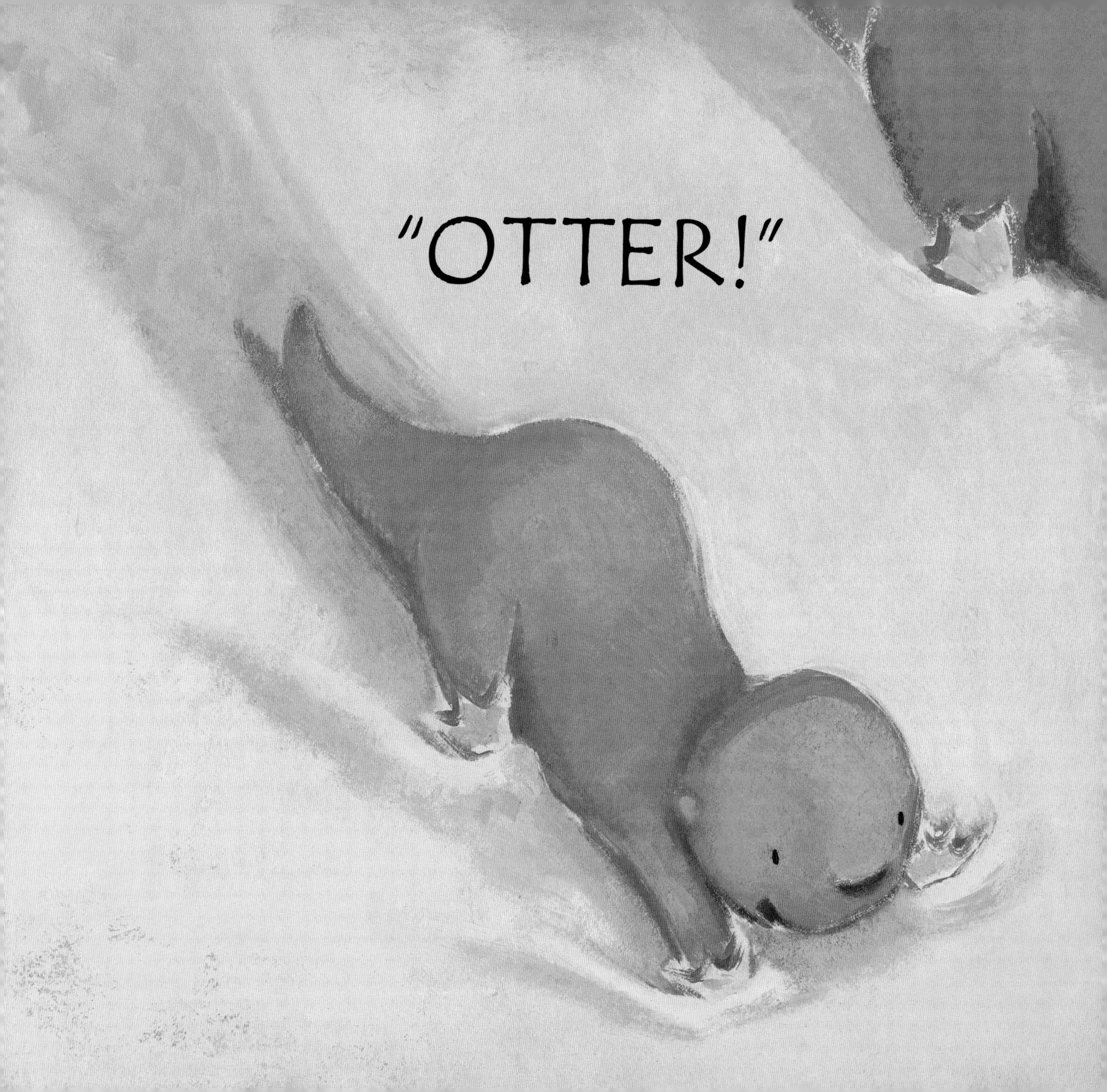

"Slide!" barks the baby otter.
"Slick, quick ride!"
So the mama helps the baby otter
sloop

slop

slide

past the purple, purple irises
blooming in the muck.

"Look!" barks the baby otter.
"I see a ...

"DUCK!"

"Paddle!" quacks the baby duck.
"Paddle and skedaddle!"
So the mama helps the baby duck
polly

wolly

paddle

through the yellow, yellow lilies
by the beaver house.

"Look!" quacks the baby duck.
"I see a ...

"MOUSE!"

"Creep!" squeaks the baby mouse.
"Don't make a peep."
So the mama helps the baby mouse
slip

slow

creep

past the pink, pink roses
all growing wild.

"Look!" squeaks the baby mouse.

"I see a ...

"CHILD!"

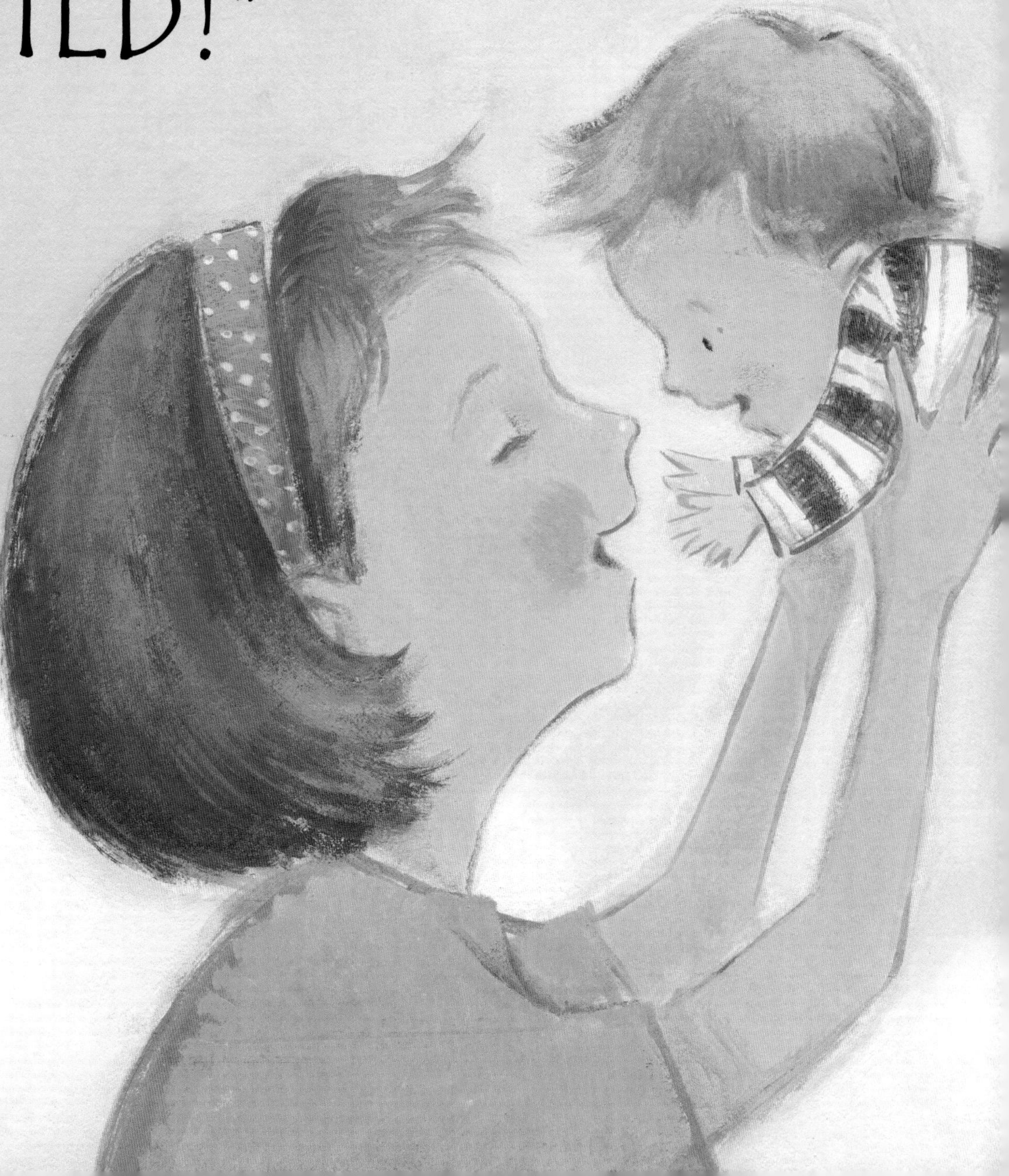

"Kiss!" says the baby child.
"Kiss, kiss, kiss!"
So the mama and the baby child
kiss like this ...

in the honey-sunny day
in the bright and breezy air.

"Look!" says the baby child...

"Babies everywhere!"

For my children, who teach me to be braver,
and for Isabella Asha, new world traveller
P. R.

Especially for Sophy, Max and Simon
D. W.

First published 2009 by Walker Books Ltd
87 Vauxhall Walk, London SE11 5HJ

10 9 8 7 6 5 4 3 2 1

Text © 2009 Phyllis Root
Illustrations © 2009 David Walker

This book has been typeset in Tempura Sans.

Printed in China

British Library Cataloguing in Publication Data
is available.

ISBN 978-1-4063-1825-8

www.walker.co.uk